The Clumsy Alligator

by June Woodman
Illustrated by Ken Morton

BRIMAX BOOKS · NEWMARKET · ENGLAND

Alligator has big feet. He has a big tail too. Sometimes he trips over his big feet. Sometimes he trips over his big tail. And sometimes he trips over everything. Then all his friends laugh. They call him the clumsy alligator.

One day Alligator is walking along when he sees Ostrich picking plums.
"Hello, Ostrich," he shouts.
But Alligator does not see the log Ostrich is standing on. He bumps into it. CRASH!
Ostrich tumbles to the ground. The bucket lands on her head.
"Oops," says Alligator.

Alligator helps take the bucket
off Ostrich's head.
"Stay away from me, Alligator,"
she cries. She gets up and runs
off over the stepping stones to
the other side of the river.
"Sorry, Ostrich," shouts Alligator.

He turns away and goes to look
for his friend Lion. He sees
him lying in the grass. Lion is
asleep as usual. Alligator
runs up to his friend.
But he does not see his tail.
He steps on it very hard.
"Aaaarr," roars Lion.

"Oops!" says Alligator.
Lion is very cross.
"You clumsy animal," says Lion.
"I am going over the river
to find a quiet place to rest."
Lion goes across the stepping
stones.
"Sorry, Lion," says Alligator.
"Stay away from me," roars Lion.

Alligator heads back to his muddy bank. His friend Spider comes to see him.
"Hey Alligator," calls Spider. "Look at my new shoes!"
Alligator waves his long tail. Bits of mud go flying through the air.

Spider starts to run but it is
too late. SPLASH!
Down comes the mud, all over
Spider's new shoes.
"Oops," says Alligator.
"Look at my new shoes,"
moans Spider.
He runs away from Alligator.
He goes across the river on the
stepping stones.

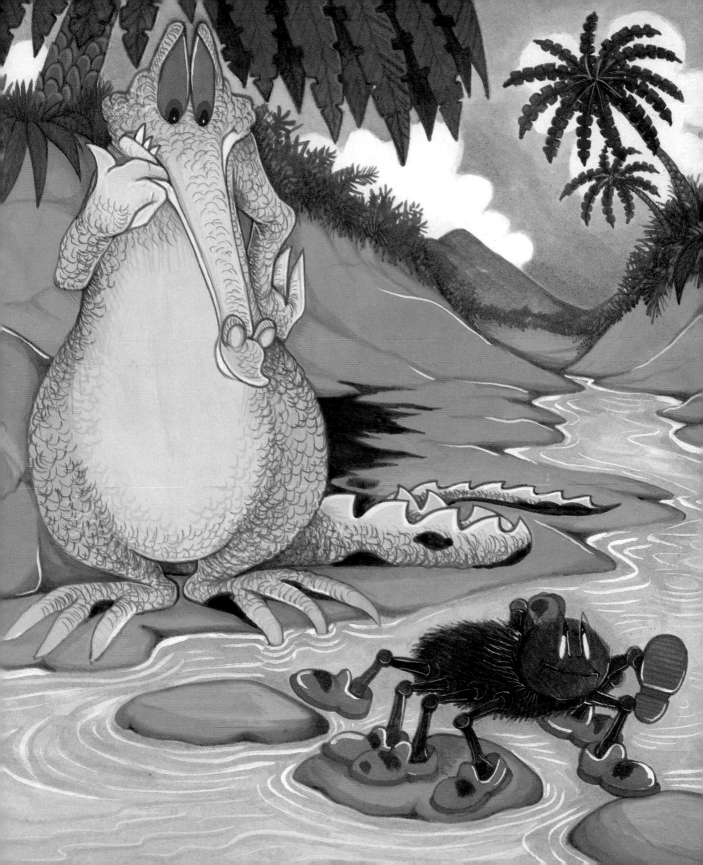

"Sorry, Spider," shouts Alligator.
"Stay away from me," cries
Spider. Alligator decides to go
and see his friend Kangaroo.
She is picking flowers with
her baby and Hippo.
"Hello," calls Alligator.
He runs up to them.
He does not see the flowers
by the path.

"Watch out," cries Hippo but it is too late. Alligator crushes all the flowers.
"Oops," says Alligator.
Baby Kangaroo starts to cry. Kangaroo picks him up and puts him into her pouch.
"Come on, Hippo," says Kangaroo. "We shall go over the river."
They cross the river on the stepping stones.

"Sorry, everyone," shouts
Alligator.
"Stay away from us," calls
Hippo.
Poor Alligator! He sits down
beside the crushed flowers.
He feels sad.
"Nobody likes me because
I spoil everything," he says.
"I wish my feet and tail were
not so big and clumsy."

The sun goes in and it gets very cold. The wind begins to blow and the raindrops start to fall.
It rains and it rains.
Soon the river is full.
Alligator can hardly see the stepping stones at all.

He sees his friends on the
other side. He runs down
to the river.
"Help! We cannot get back!"
they all cry.
"I can help," says Alligator.
He steps into the river. He digs
two big feet into one bank,
and two big feet into the other.
"Jump on," he calls.

One by one, the animals step onto Alligator's tail and walk across his back to the other side of the river.
"Three cheers for Alligator," says Kangaroo when all the animals are safely across.
"We are very pleased to have a friend with such big feet and such a big tail."
Alligator smiles a very big smile.

Here are some words in the story.

trips	mud
clumsy	flowers
picking	crushes
plums	digs
tail	bank
quiet	jump
waves	smile